This book belongs to:

For my father Sri, who taught me the joy of reading from the seat of his sarong.
Diwa

For Livia, my sister: always together to recreate the magic of our childhood garden.
Nerina

First published in the United Kingdom in 2018 by Lantana Publishing Ltd., London.
www.lantanapublishing.com

American edition published in 2018 by Lantana Publishing Ltd., UK.
info@lantanapublishing.com

A CIP catalogue record for this book is available from the British Library.

Distributed in the United States and Canada by Lerner Publishing Group, Inc.
241 First Avenue North, Minneapolis, MN 55401 U.S.A.
For reading levels and more information, look for this title at www.lernerbooks.com.
Cataloging-in-Publication Data Available.

Printed and bound in Hong Kong.

ISBN: 978-1-911373-22-3
eBook ISBN: 978-1-911373-23-0

Kaya's Heart Song

Diwa Tharan Sanders

& Nerina Canzi

“Mama, what are you singing?” asks Kaya as Mama sits humming to herself.

“That was my heart song. Happy hearts have their own songs,” says Mama with a wink. “Let me tell you a secret – if you have a heart song, anything is possible. Even magic!”

“But I don’t know my heart song, Mama,” says Kaya.

“Yes you do, my dear, you just have to learn to listen for it.”

Kaya sits down to listen. But she doesn’t hear anything at all.

“When the time is right, you’ll hear it. Learn to quieten your mind so the music can be heard,” says Mama with a knowing smile.

“Now, why don’t you go outside and play?”

Kaya leaves Mama and runs towards the jungle. She skips along the path she knows so well.

A butterfly appears next to her.

“Hello pretty butterfly! Are you leading me somewhere?” Kaya jokes.

They come to a small wooden hut.

“I’ve not been in this part of the jungle before,” Kaya says.

She spots someone she knows from the village.

“Good Afternoon, Pak!” she calls out.

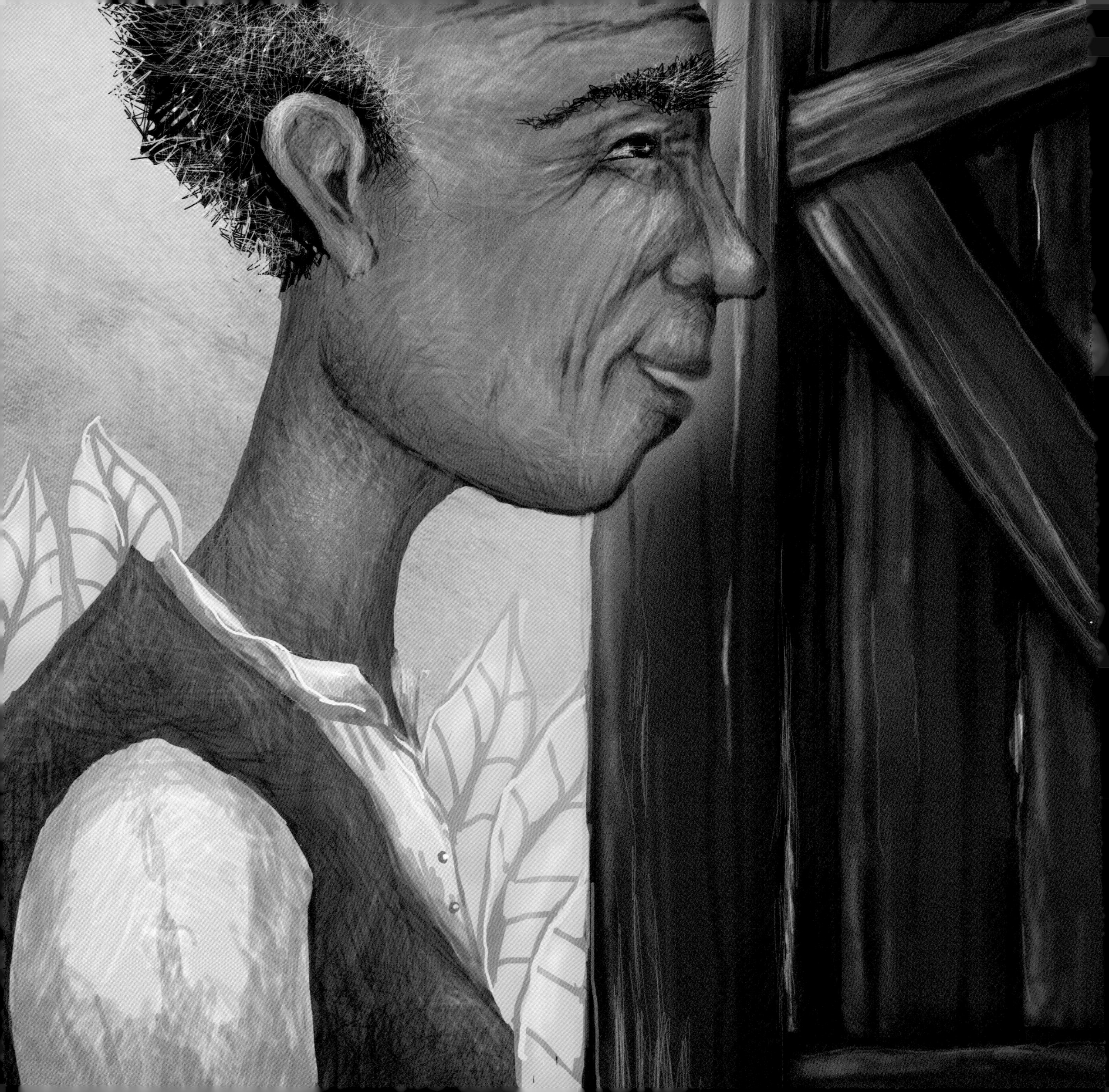

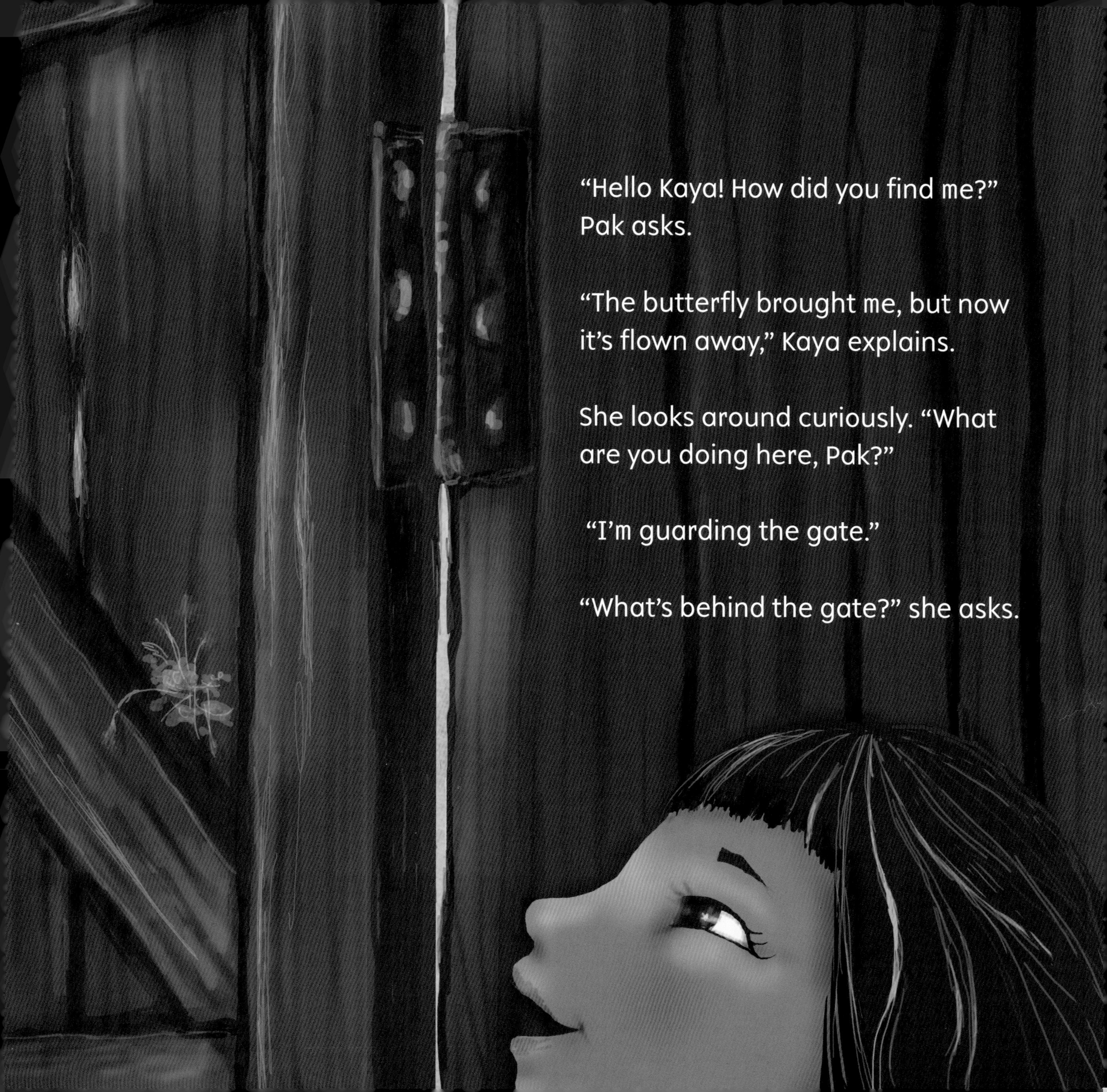

“Hello Kaya! How did you find me?” Pak asks.

“The butterfly brought me, but now it’s flown away,” Kaya explains.

She looks around curiously. “What are you doing here, Pak?”

“I’m guarding the gate.”

“What’s behind the gate?” she asks.

It’s an elephant carousel!

Oooooo....!

It’s the most beautiful carousel
Kaya has ever seen.

But here in the jungle, it looks
unused, unloved and forgotten.

“It’s broken,” Pak says sadly.

Kaya hops onto one of
the elephants.

She begins to uncurl
the vines from the
elephants' sides.

While her fingers busy themselves, she imagines herself as a princess riding her elephant down the jungle paths.

Her mind quietens and becomes very still.

A soft beat begins to whisper in her ear. She finds herself swaying to its rhythm.

Suddenly, she feels the carousel turning.

"Waaaaaah – hoooo!
We're moving!"

Pak's eyes are as wide as saucers. He jumps on too!

The elephants begin to move in time to the music.

Boom taktak boom taktak boom

Shick shak shook

Boom taktak boom taktak boom

Shick shak shook...

Kaya’s heart beats along and all of a sudden she knows what it is.

“It’s my heart song, I can hear it!” she cries.

Boom taktak boom taktak boom
Shick shak shook
Boom taktak boom taktak boom
Shick shak shook

There is a rustling in the bushes. The butterfly is back! And this time, it's not alone.

"Mama was right!" says Kaya gleefully. "If you have a heart song, anything is possible!"

There is magic in the air.
And elephant rides for everyone!

As the carousel slows, the elephants curtsey and Kaya's heart song gently fades away.

"Thank you, Kaya, for bringing magic to my carousel," says Pak.

"And thank you, Pak, for helping me find my heart song. I promise to share it for all to hear."

And she does.

Mindfulness

To practice mindfulness is to experience a kind of magic, much like finding your heart song. When the mind quietens and comes into stillness, there is room for awareness to move in. The breath slows, the body relaxes, thoughts calm down, and we stop being and just *be*. It is in this state of '*be*-ing' that we find ourselves completely present in what is real for us at that very moment. The past and the future are forgotten and our focus rests solely on the *now*. We welcome thoughts, emotions and feelings without resisting them or reacting to them. In this *be*-ing state, the doors to self-awareness open.

Meditation and yoga are ways to explore this *be*-ingness of the mind. At the beginning of our story, Mama sits in a cross-legged meditation position humming her heart song. Meditation brings awareness to the mind and body, which is similar to the awareness that comes through practicing yoga. In yoga, we move through different *asanas*, or postures, often guided by the breath. Paying attention to the breath is one way to come into a mindful state.

When Kaya frees the elephants from the vines that have grown around them, she discovers that doing something with full awareness can also bring us to a mindful state.

We invite you to explore mindfulness and find ways to bring it into your life.

Everyone has a heart song. What's yours?